Tell Me About Your Day Today

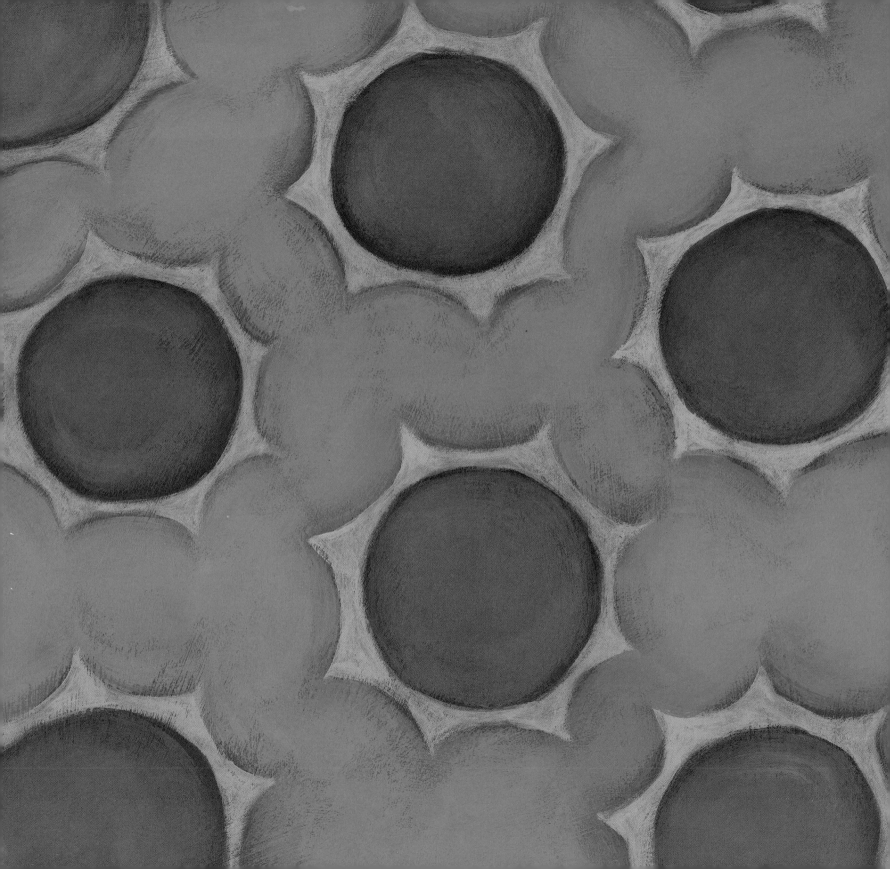

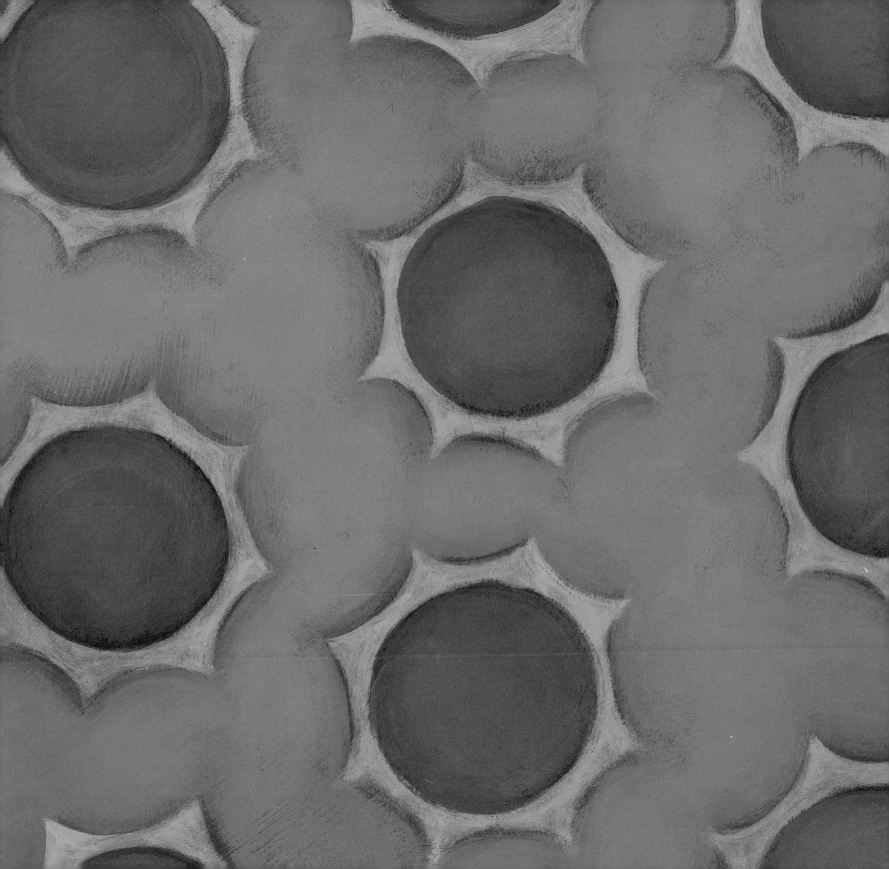

For Joelie
—M F

For Anne Ylvisaker, my story-sharing friend,
and for M., R., and C., my storytelling family
—L S

Special thanks to my husband, Matthew Smith,
for always arriving to my studio just in time with patience, insight, and encouragement.
And more special thanks to my Beach Lane editors,
Allyn Johnston and Andrea Welch,
who work wonders with scissors and glue sticks!
—L S

ISBN 978-0-545-64769-4

12 11 10 9 8 7 6 5 4 3 2 1   13 14 15 16 17 18/0

Printed in the U.S.A.

First Scholastic printing, September 2013   40

Book design by Lauren Rille
The text for this book is set in Colwell.
The illustrations for this book are rendered in acrylic paint on gessoed Arches 140-lb. hot press watercolor paper.

Tell Me About Your Day Today

by Mem Fox • illustrated by Lauren Stringer

SCHOLASTIC INC.

There was once a boy who loved bedtime.

He loved the last kiss.

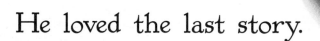

He loved the last story.

He loved the last good night.

He knew he was in the company
of friends and couldn't wait
for their conversation
to begin.

Greedy Goose coughed a little cough.

"Hello, Greedy Goose," the boy whispered. He *loved* Greedy Goose. "Tell me about your day today."

And Greedy Goose
told him about her day~

the who,

the what,

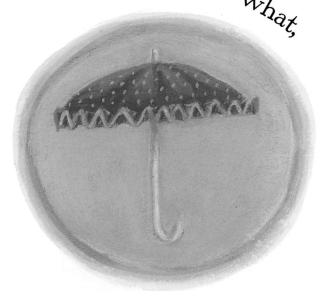

the why,

and the way . . .

the whole wild thing . . .

turned out okay.

Then Blue Horse shook her mane.
"Hello, Blue Horse," the boy whispered.
He *loved* Blue Horse. "Tell me about your
day today."

And Blue Horse told
him about her day~

the who,

the what,

the why,

and the way . . .

the whole wild thing . . .

turned out okay.

Next Fat Rabbit twitched his ears. "Hello, Fat Rabbit," the boy whispered. He *loved* Fat Rabbit. "Tell me about your day today."

And Fat Rabbit told
him about his day~

the who,

the what,

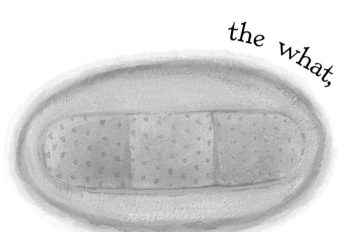

the why,

and the way . . .

the whole wild thing . . .

turned out okay.

"But how about you?"
Greedy Goose asked.
"Tell us about *your* day today."

And so the boy looked back . . .

on the who,

the what,

and the way

the why,

their whole wild day . . .

turned out okay!

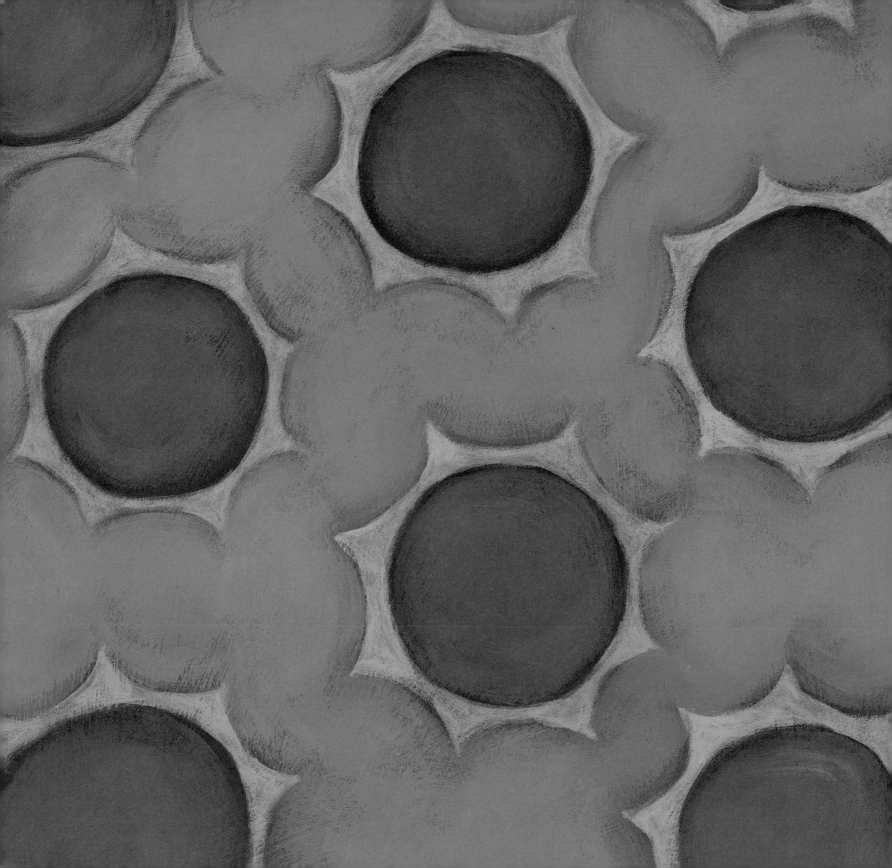

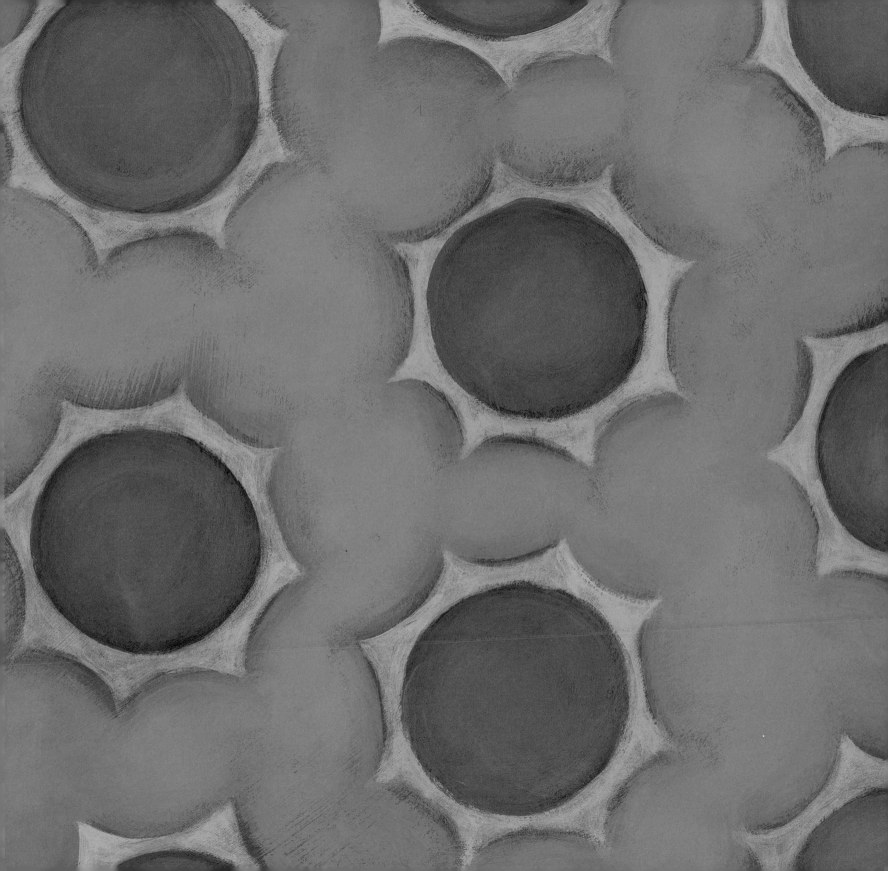